James an Queen of Sodor

**Based on *The Railway Series*
by The Rev. W. Awdry**

James thought he was the most important engine on the Island of Sodor. He was very proud of his shiny red paintwork, which he kept clean and smart so he was always ready to do important jobs for The Fat Controller.

One day, Percy joined James and Gordon at the washdown. He had been working at the Quarry, so he was very dirty.

"My whistle's all clogged up," he said. He blew hard to clear it, and accidentally covered Gordon in mud!

"Don't get me dirty, too," said James. "I've got to stay nice and clean because I'm going to collect the mayor!"

Soon James had picked up the mayor and was puffing proudly across the Island. When he passed Gordon, he whistled loudly to show off. Gordon was not amused. He decided he had to teach James a lesson.

That afternoon, The Fat Controller needed an engine to take the Queen of Sodor to the scrap yard.

"She is a leaky old barge, so it's a very dirty job!" he said.

Just then, James arrived at the shed. Gordon knew he hated getting dirty, so he decided to trick him.

"That's a *very* important job," he said.

"An important job?" said James quickly. "I will do that!"

James felt very proud when he heard he would be collecting the Queen of Sodor. He thought the other engines must be very jealous. His paintwork was shiny and clean, and he could hardly wait to meet the Queen.

Before long, James arrived at the canal.
"I'm here to collect the Queen of Sodor,"
he announced, proudly.
The manager pointed to a dirty old barge.
"There she is," he said.
"Oh, no! The Queen's a slimy old barge!"
James said in horror.

James realised Gordon had tricked
him into doing the dirty job.
"He wants me to get all mucky!"
he said.
James was more determined than
ever that he would deliver the barge
without getting dirty.

"Watch out!" called his Driver, as
he applied the brakes.
Luckily, James managed to stop just
in time. Oil slopped over the barge, but
James stayed clean. Workmen came
and fixed the pipe and James carried
on his journey.

James was very relieved to leave the dirty barge at the scrap yard. When he arrived back at the engine shed, the engines were surprised to see him still looking clean.

"How did you stay so clean?" asked Thomas in surprise.

"I *have* to stay clean," replied James, "so I'm always ready to do important jobs."

Just then, Percy returned from working at the Quarry.

"My whistle is clogged again," he said. He blew hard to clear it, and this time he covered James in dust!

"No!" cried James, but it was too late. He had managed to stay clean all day and now he was filthy!

James sighed loudly.

"I hope there aren't any important jobs to do," teased Thomas. "You would definitely need a washdown first, James." The engines all peeped cheerfully and even James smiled in the end!